For Old Brown.
Wherever you may be.

Pig the Slob was first published in Australia in 2020 by Scholastic Press,
an imprint of Scholastic Australia Pty Ltd., under the title *Pig the Blob*.

ISBN 978-1-338-73022-7

12 11 10 9 8 7 6 5 4 3 2 1   20 21 22 23 24 25

Printed in the U.S.A.   76

This edition first printing, September 2020

The artwork in this book is acrylic (with pens and pencils) on watercolor paper.
The type was set in Adobe Caslon.

Aaron Blabey

SCHOLASTIC INC.

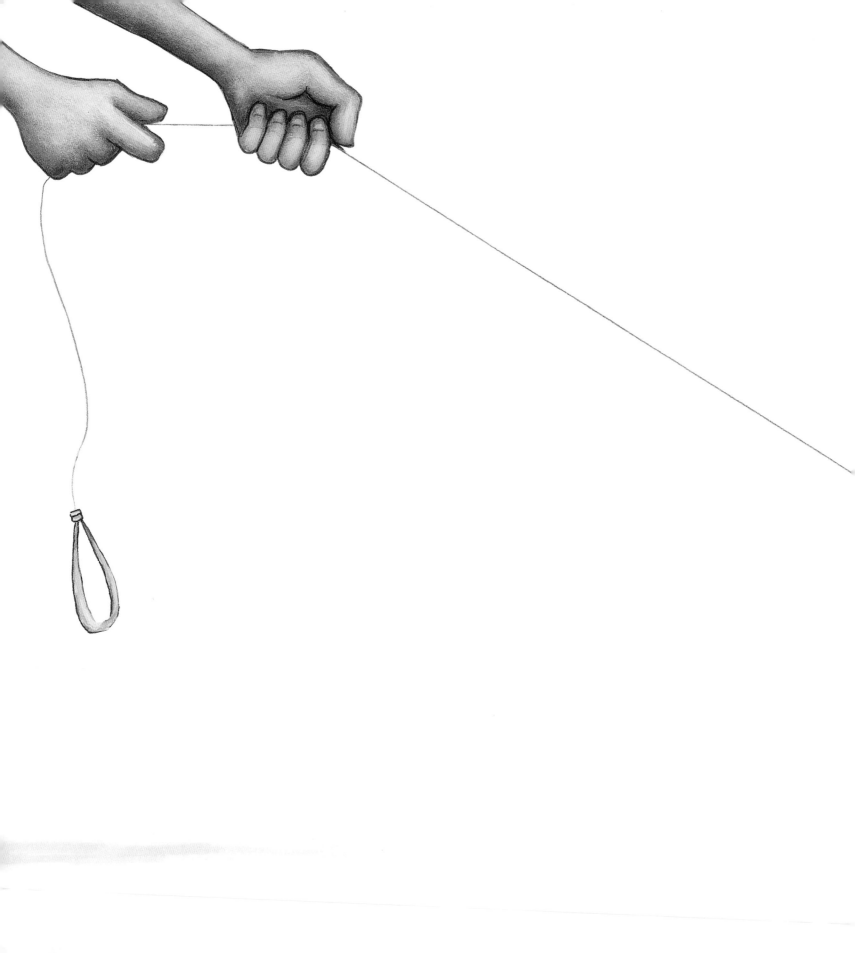

Pig was a pug
and I'm sorry to say,
he was *shockingly* lazy.
Such a shameful display . . .

He lived in a flat . . .

. . . horizontal position,
which left him in truly
appalling condition.

Full of candy and soda
and thick mozzarella,
Pig was a hard-core,
full-time sofa dweller.

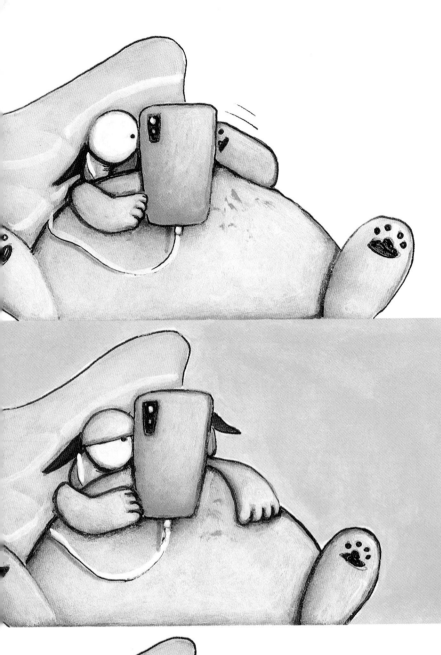

His only exertion
was swiping a screen —

SWIPE . . .

STARE . . .

REPEAT . . .

was his grueling routine.

Sure, once in a while
he would lift a remote.
But it made him quite tired,
and his ankles would bloat.

Flat on his back
he'd relax with a sigh,
bingeing on TV
and nuggets and pie.

Pig dug in deep.
He was *part of the couch*.
An immovable lump
in a warm, sticky pouch.

Trevor was worried —
Pig's health was at risk!
"We should take a quick jog . . .
or a walk, nice and brisk!"

Pig stirred from his stupor.
His reply was quite tart.
He simply said, "No."
And then unleashed a . . .

"We'd have so much fun though!"
tried Trevor once more.

SLAP!

It was a suggestion
Pig chose to ignore.

From a bunker of sloth
and with no sense of shame,
Pig returned to his ice cream
and video game.

And that's when they heard it . . .

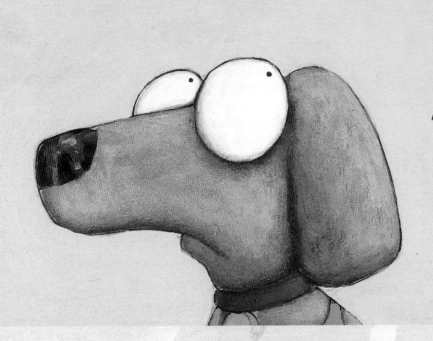

Trev stopped in his tracks.

"What's groaning?" asked Pig
through a mouthful of snacks.

The first groan was subtle . . .

AAAAAAAAAAANNNNNNNNNN

The next one was not . . .

The *floorboards* were GROANING!

Yes, groaning a LOT.

"Could that be my tummy?"
asked Pig, blinking slow.

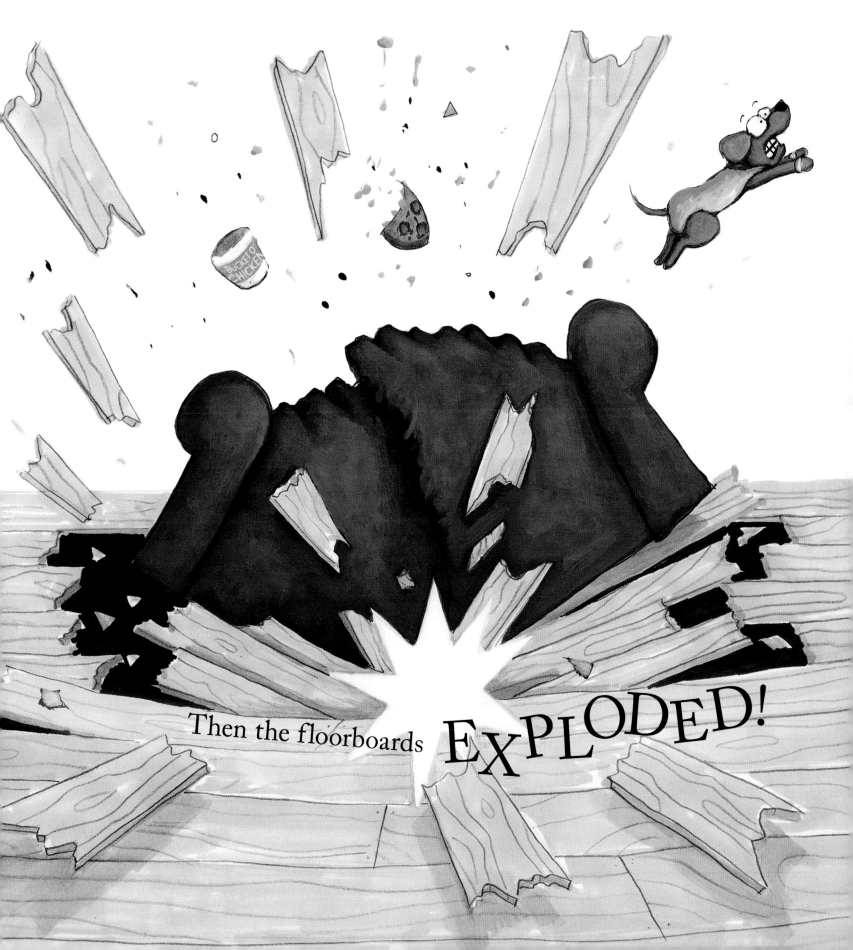

Then the floorboards EXPLODED!

Hey! Watch

out below!

These days it's different,
I'm happy to say.
Pig makes an effort
to come out and play.

He's up off the couch
doing cartwheels and squats!
He practices yoga
and goes jogging LOTS!

His workouts are GREAT!
But the part he likes best,
is when he gets home . . .

. . . he can have a nice rest.